Églantine

Véronique

Jessamine

Rose

Delphine

Verveine

For Magda and Clare Marcus
— Mary Hoffman

For my parents
— Miss Clara

The Twelve Dancing Princesses

Amandine

Retold by Mary Hoffman
Illustrated by Miss Clara
Narrated by Xanthe Gresham

Barefoot Books
step inside a story

Once upon a time, there was a king who had twelve
beautiful daughters. The king and the queen rejoiced in their good
fortune. To each daughter, they gave the name of a flower — there was
Violette, Delphine, Iris, Jessamine, Lilou, Véronique and Verveine,
Eglantine, Amarante, Marguerite, Rose and Amandine. But when the last
princess was born, the queen fell gravely ill. Before she died, she turned
to her grieving husband. "Take care of our girls, my dearest," she said.
'They will need a lot of looking after as they get older."

How right she was! By the time the eldest, Princess
Violette, was eighteen, the palace was swarming with suitors.
They were all the younger sons of other kings, hoping
to gain a crown as well as a wife.

The king was very fond of his daughters and he wanted
them all to find good husbands. But he had a terrible problem,
and try as he might, he could not solve it. He had given the princesses
a large and lofty chamber in one of the wings of the palace. Every evening
he would come and say good night and then leave the princesses to get ready to
go to sleep. He would close the door quietly behind him and turn the key in
the lock to make sure the princesses stayed there till morning.

But every morning the princesses' beautiful silk and satin slippers had
been reduced to rags and tatters. Obviously, they had been out dancing —
but where? And how? And who with? The palace was kept firmly
bolted and guarded at night and any stray princes were swiftly
sent out into the courtyard as soon as darkness fell.

The three palace shoemakers
were kept busy every day making fresh slippers
for the twelve princesses. Every evening, new slippers were
placed in their bedchamber, but every morning, the maids who came
to wake the princesses found the slippers worn to rags.
Every mouse in the palace knew she could find nice soft scraps of material
to line her nest if she visited the princesses' bedroom in the morning.
There were silks and satins of every hue, pattern and texture, and
ribbons and tassels that had come loose.

The king was frantic. His daughters were pale and yawning, just as if they
had danced the night away, and their ruined slippers told the same
story. But when he asked them what had happened, they
merely shook their sleepy heads as if under
some enchantment.

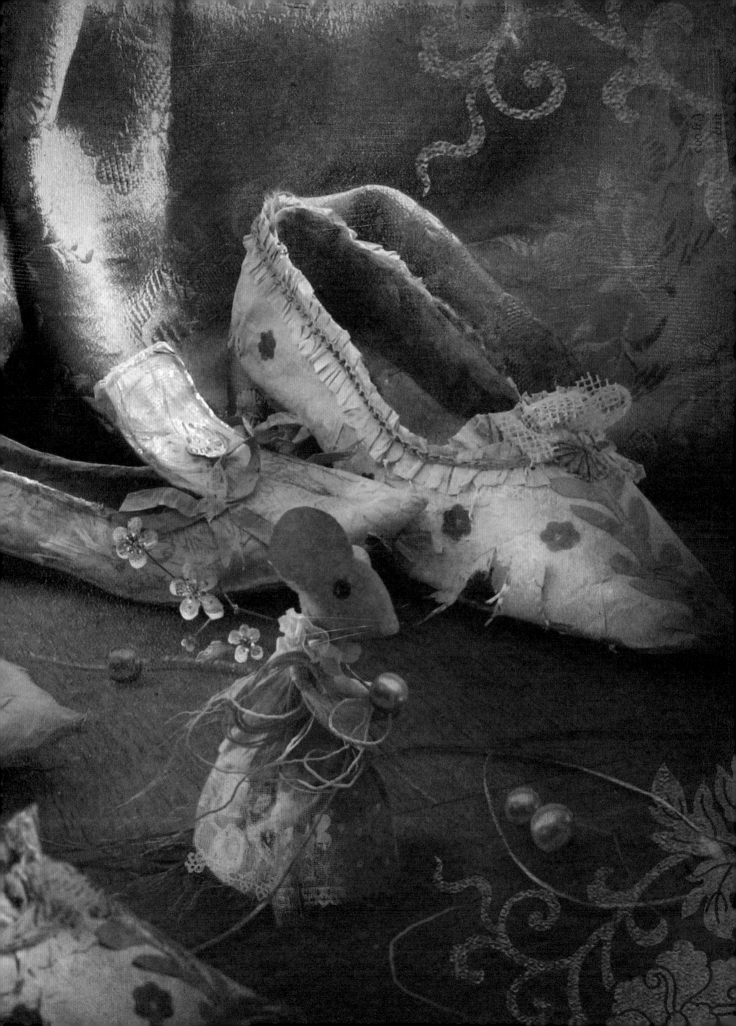

Well, if this was magic, the king decided he would
beat it with cunning. He issued a proclamation:

His Majesty the King

Every unwedded man with wisdom an
courage is hereby invited to prese
himself at the palace.
The first man to discover where
daughters go dancing eac
be free to choose his brid
hand in marriage of o
and to inher

elve
ght will
sk for the

the princesses
y kingdom.

eware: should anyone try for
ee nights but find out nothing, on
e third morning, he will lose his life.

Nov. 15. 1739.

The first prince tried the very next
night. He was given the room opposite the
princesses' bedroom to sleep in. Their room
was left open but, since the prince planned
to stay on watch all night, he thought it
would be impossible for princesses to creep
past him and to leave the castle.

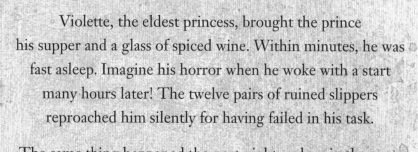

Violette, the eldest princess, brought the prince
his supper and a glass of spiced wine. Within minutes, he was
fast asleep. Imagine his horror when he woke with a start
many hours later! The twelve pairs of ruined slippers
reproached him silently for having failed in his task.

The same thing happened the next night and again the next.

On the third day, the prince was dispatched.

And so it went on; the palace was
soon remarkably empty of young
men hoping for a crown and a bride.

Now it happened that one day a soldier came limping along the road.
He had taken a wound in the wars and been discharged from the army.
As he rested by the roadside to eat his meager lunch, an old
woman hobbled up and asked if he could spare any food.
"Of course, ma'am," he said politely.
"You are welcome to half of all I have."

When they had finished, the old woman said, "Thank you,
kind sir. Would it not be good to have a warm bed for life,
as much food as you could eat and a beautiful young wife?"

"It would be wonderful," said the soldier. "But I'd need a fairy
to wave her wand to give me that good fortune."

The old woman straightened up, and the soldier thought
she looked younger than before. She told him the riddle
of the princesses and their worn out shoes. "The king has
offered his kingdom and the hand in marriage of one of the
princesses to anyone who can solve the mystery," she finished.
"You have helped me and I can see you are brave and good.
Do what I am about to tell you and you will
succeed where others have not."

The old lady told the soldier he must
not eat or drink anything the princesses offered.
Then she gave him a silky cloth folded as small as a hankerchief.
"When you put this cloak on it will make you invisible.
You can follow the princesses unseen." As she waved good-bye, the
strange old woman stood straight and regal. "The queen's good wishes
go with you," she said, "just remember not to drink the wine."

The king gave the soldier just as warm
a welcome as the young princes had received —
and some smart new clothes as well.

"He is handsome," whispered little Princess Amandine,
peeping out from behind a screen.

"But he can't be a prince," said Princess Violette.
"A prince would have come by carriage. I saw him limping
up the palace steps like a poor weary traveler."

That night, Princess Violette brought spiced
wine to the soldier but she did not see him tip it
away in a potted palm. Soon he was yawning and
stretching and rubbing his eyes. "This one is not
even going to try," sighed Violette as she and
her sisters heard the soldier's snores.

"Sleep well, handsome stranger," she called softly.
"See you in the morning."
Then she turned to the other princesses.
"Come, sisters — let's get ready!" she laughed.

All twelve princesses opened the chests that contained
their finest clothes and dressed themselves in silk and satins
and lace. They wound colored ribbons and shimmering pearls
in their hair, picked up fans and flowers, adjusted their coronets
of silver and gold, sprayed one another with expensive perfumes
and, finally, slid their dainty feet into brand new slippers of green
and lavender and blue, to match their elaborate dresses.

Princess Violette went to the corner of her bed and tapped
the floor with her elegant purple slipper — one, two, three.

But the soldier was not asleep; he was watching from his
room, every nerve in his body tingling. And as soon as
the eldest princess tapped the floor, he saw her bed swing
away to reveal a stone staircase. He flung the magic cloak
over his head and followed the disappearing girls.

He was so quick on their heels as they were
descending deep below the castle that he trod on the
hem of Princess Amandine's lemon taffeta dress.
"Oh!" cried Amandine. "Who is there?" And she sounded
so frightened that all the princesses stopped and turned
to see what was the matter.

"No one," said her big sister, Princess Violette. She had looked out
for Amandine ever since their mother died. "You are imagining it.
Come on, we must go quickly." She took Amandine's hand.
The stone staircase led down and down and out through the
cellars of the castle into a wood, where the princesses
slipped through the trees like a flock of butterflies.

The soldier followed them. The trees in the wood
glowed silver in the moonlight. "I'd better take back
a twig," thought the soldier "so that the king will believe me."
Crack! The twig of silver leaves snapped off so loudly that the littlest
princess turned round, startled. But her eldest sister grabbed her hand
and hurried her on, into another wood. The soldier followed silently.
Here the trees had leaves of gold and the princesses poured through
the golden wood like a procession of rainbows. Again, the soldier
snapped off a twig and again, the eldest princess had to
reassure her littlest sister when she jumped at the sound.

On the princesses glided, and behind them limped the soldier,
as fast and as noiselessly as he could. They came to a third wood
where all the leaves on the trees were made of sparkling diamonds.
They tinkled like a million crystal chandeliers as the princesses
swept passed them, brushing them with their beautiful
multi-colored dresses. The soldier watched the fluttering
princesses make their way like a shower of shooting stars.

He took a twig of diamond leaves that made a sound
like a little chime of bells as he stowed it in his jacket
with the other twigs. The littlest princess
looked up but, by then, they had reached
the edge of a lake and her sisters
were all hurrying her along.

Drawn up at the edge of the lake were
twelve slender boats, with a prince sitting in each of them.
Across the other side of the water gleamed a castle made
of white marble, shining with so many lights that
the darkness of the night was banished.

The soldier watched amazed as each princess stepped into a
boat and was rowed away. Just as the last boat left, the soldier
stepped into it, unseen under his cloak. It was the boat that
Princess Amandine sat in and she shivered as the boat rocked.
"You are heavier than usual," teased the youngest prince.
"What have you been eating?"

When the boats reached the other side
of the lake, the princes jumped out and escorted
the princesses into a ballroom sparkling with lights and
tingling with music.

The soldier stood and watched the dancing through his cloak,
as the nimble-footed princes in their fine velvets and brocades
whisked and whirled the twelve princesses round the ballroom.

The princesses danced every dance, until the soldier
could see their slippers unravelling in strips.
Then he knew it was time to go home.

This time, the soldier stepped into the eldest princess's
boat so that he could run ahead of them all through the enchanted
woods and back up the stone stairs and hurl himself into bed,
with the cloak of invisibility stuffed under his pillow.

"Ah, see — there is nothing to worry about," said Princess Violette,
as the princesses climbed the last stone stair and slid the bed back
over the magic door. She peeped into the soldier's bedroom.
"Look — there's our brave soldier! He is fast asleep in his bed."
The soldier smiled to himself but lay as still as stone;
he had solved the riddle.

For the next two nights, everything
happened in exactly the same way, with the
mysterious staircase, the journey through the three
woods and across the lake, the dancing and feasting
in the castle and the shoes worn out before dawn.

But on the third night, as he left the ballroom
for the last time, the soldier took a golden wine
goblet from the table and hid it in his jacket.

All that evening, Princess Amandine had been
nervous, looking around her as if she could sense
the soldier's presence. From the corner of her eye,
she saw the golden cup suddenly vanish. She was very
afraid but she bravely kept her fears to herself.

At the end of the night, as dawn was beginning to creep
across the sky, the soldier ran ahead as fast as he could,
limping as he always did, up the stone stairs to his bed.
His heart was thumping knowing that in the morning
he must convince the king or die.

"My daughters sail to an enchanted castle
each night?" said the king the next day. "And dance
with princes who are under a spell?"

"Yes, Your Majesty," replied the soldier. "They climb down
a staircase under the palace and travel through
magic woods of silver, gold and diamonds."
He laid the three twigs of precious metals and gems in front of the king.
"Then they are rowed across the lake and dance all night in the castle," he went on.

The soldier took the golden goblet from his jacket. He put that on
the table too. Just then, there was a gasp and a rustle of silk from the next
room and they both knew the princesses were listening. The king knew
the soldier was telling the truth. "You have solved my problem at
long last," he said. "Which of my daughters will you have?"
"The eldest," said the soldier. "Princess Violette will
will suit me very well. She is always kind to her youngest
sister and I hope she'll be kind to me."

That night there was
a grand ball in the king's palace, just as
glittering as any ever held in the enchanted castle. This
time, the soldier needed no magic cloak of invisibility and he
danced as if he had never hurt his leg in the war. The king danced
with each of his daughters in turn until his own shoes were worn out.

All the princes who were left in the kingdom came to the ball, but
nothing more was ever heard of the ones under a spell in the castle
across the lake. And no one ever found the staircase again; it
was sealed up forever once the riddle of the dancing
princesses had been solved.

Barefoot Books
2067 Massachusetts Ave
Cambridge, MA 02140

Adapted from the fairy tale by the Brothers Grimm
Text copyright © 2012 by Mary Hoffman
Illustrations by Miss Clara, first published in France as
La Bal des douze princesses © Hachette-Livre / Gautier-Languereau, 2011
The moral rights of Mary Hoffman and Miss Clara have been asserted
Story CD narrated by Xanthe Gresham
Recorded, mixed and mastered by Sans Walk Spoken Word Studio, England

First published in the United States of America by Barefoot Books, Inc in 2012
This hardback edition with story CD first published in 2013
All rights reserved

Graphic design by Louise Millar, London
Color separation by B&P International, Hong Kong
Printed in China on 100% acid-free paper
This book was typeset in Carlton, Escrita, Zapfino and Janson
The illustrations were prepared as scale models,
which were photographed and digitally enhanced

ISBN 978-1-84686-966-2

Library of Congress Cataloging-in-Publication Data
is available under 2012009598

1 3 5 7 9 8 6 4 2

Mary Hoffman

has three beautiful daughters who all like dancing. As well as raising daughters, she has written nearly a hundred books, which is far less tiring! Mary lives close to Oxford, UK. *The Twelve Dancing Princesses* has always been one of her favorite stories.
www.maryhoffman.co.uk

Miss Clara

is an artist who creates enchanting and mysterious worlds. She builds miniature maquettes of princesses, hobgoblins and other magical characters out of paper, and detailed scenes in which to photograph them. She adds fine details digitally. Miss Clara lives in Bordeaux, France.
www.missclara.com

Xanthe Gresham

used to save her bus fare to school by walking through the park, memorizing beautiful things. She is now an acclaimed writer and storyteller who the Arts Council of England described as "speaking like a woman spitting jewels." Xanthe lives in Sussex, UK.
www.xanthegresham.co.uk